SNUFFY AND VROOM-VROOM

Written by Elizabeth Lavine

Illustrated by Sheila McGraw

SNUFFY AND VROOM-VROOM

Written and published by Elizabeth Lavine

Illustrated by Sheila McGraw

Copyright 2013 © Elizabeth Lavine for the text

Copyright 2013 © Sheila McGraw for the illustrations

ISBN-13: 978-1481286664

ISBN-10: 1481286668

For Jean, Jenny and Matt.

Once upon a time, two vacuum cleaners lived in a store. They were brothers—Snuffy and Vroom-Vroom. Snuffy was orange, and Vroom-Vroom was green.

At night when the store closed, they laughed, whispered and wondered about all sorts of things. Mostly, they wondered who would take them home.

What an exciting day that would be!

One day, a man came to the store. He was in a great hurry to buy a vacuum cleaner, so he grabbed Vroom-Vroom and rushed off.

Snuffy was shocked and upset that he was left behind. He had always thought that Vroom-Vroom and he would go to the same home and be together forever.

Snuffy was sad and lonely all night long.

The next morning, a family came shopping. They stopped in front of Snuffy.

Audrey, the older girl, patted Snuffy. "I like this one," she said.

"That's a sad-looking vacuum," Mom said.

Dad said, "Yes, but look—it's on sale!"

"Please, Mom," begged Audrey. "Can we get it? It has a turbo brush."

Snuffy, touched by Audrey's interest, felt better. Mom gave in, and they all decided to buy him.

At his new home, Snuffy was busy every day. He brushed carpets, polished floors, and vacuumed dust bunnies.

But every night, tucked in his cozy broom closet, he cried as if his heart would break. He missed his brother, Vroom-Vroom.

Late one night, a tooth fairy flew into the house. It was almost morning and she was on her way home, with one last stop to make.

She heard crying, and found Snuffy. "What's wrong, little friend? Is your bag too full? Is your cord in a knot?"

"No," Snuffy hiccupped through his tears. "I miss my brother. He's gone, and I may never see him again."

The fairy smiled kindly. "My good fellow, most every vacuum cleaner lives apart from his brother or sister. Didn't you know?"

"No," said Snuffy. "Apart?"

"Oh, my," she said. "You must have ended up in the same store. What good luck! And how long were you there together?"

"More than a year," said Snuffy.

"Oh, dear," said the fairy. "I see why you're crying. But don't feel sad; everything's going to be all right."

She flew three times in a circle, sprinkling fairy dust on him as she sweetly sang:

Vroom-Vroom's in your heart forever,
For one whole year you were together,
Kindly care for all your friends,
'Til true love brings him back again.

"But I don't have any friends," he said.

Kitty-cat meowed and raised his paw to touch Snuffy.

"That can't be," she said tenderly. "Kitty-cat is right here. And who else do you live with?"

"Mom, Dad, two little girls—"

"Good! Mom, Dad, two little girls, Kitty-cat… and what about the carpets, the floors, and the dust bunnies?"

"How are they my friends?"

"They share your life too, don't they?"

He nodded.

"Then they are your friends."

Snuffy was astonished. Could she be right? Friends all around in plain sight? He felt his sadness melting away.

"The two little girls you mentioned—is one of them Audrey, by chance?" asked the fairy.

"Yes," he said, surprised.

"Why, that's the very child I'm looking for! I have a tooth to pick up. I must hurry!"

Snuffy watched as the fairy flew off to Audrey's room and then into the night.

"Do your best!" Her voice faded away.

"I will!" Snuffy sang out.

From that day on, Snuffy was open-hearted and kind to everyone he met. He treated them as good friends. The rugs felt his gentle touch. The floors felt his happy wheels. He gave good cheer to everyone, even the dust bunnies. He finished the cleaning in record time.

The whole family was amazed.

Then one day, it was Audrey's turn to vacuum. Snuffy spotted a button on the floor. He froze.

During his time at the store, he had heard, "Be very, very careful; never vacuum a small, hard thing." All the vacuum cleaners had said so.

Snuffy noticed that baby Claire was nearby. If he left the button lying there, she might put it in her mouth. She could choke!

Snuffy knew that if Vroom-Vroom was here, *he* would vacuum that button. *He* would protect Claire, no matter what.

Snuffy's wheels and turbo brush whirred as he vacuumed the button. There was a dreadful clanging noise.

Audrey burst into tears.

Mom quickly unplugged Snuffy and hugged Audrey. "It's okay," she said. "We can take him to be fixed as good as new."

Snuffy breathed a sigh of relief, glad for his loving friends: Audrey, Mom, Dad, baby Claire, and Kitty-cat.

Mom bundled the girls into the car and placed Snuffy in the trunk. Off they went to the Just Rite Repair Shop.

Dave, the repair man, looked Snuffy over. "I see your vacuum cleaner ran over a button," he said. "No problem. I'll have it fixed as good as new by morning."

Snuffy felt the soothing comfort of Dave's gentle hands. He didn't even mind that he was going to stay overnight, away from home.

The next morning, Mom and the girls came to get Snuffy. Just as Mom was paying the bill, a man came into the store carrying a green vacuum cleaner. He flung it onto the counter.

"Can you fix this?" he demanded. "I tell you, it's a piece of junk."

"It looks like a good machine to me," said Dave, cheerfully. Carefully, he untangled the cord and loosened the clogged brush. "I'm surprised it could run at all, though—when it's been treated so badly."

"Well, keep it, then. It's been nothing but trouble to me!" said the man as he stomped from the store.

Snuffy, hanging on to every word, quivered with joy—because the vacuum cleaner on the counter was his brother, Vroom-Vroom!

"Why, it's just like our wonderful vacuum cleaner," said Mom, "which in the past few weeks has been unbelievable! It practically cleans our house by itself."

Dave shook his head. "Hmm… let me turn it on to see if it's even fixable." He plugged in Vroom-Vroom and the vacuum gave a little cough.

"Well, I'll be," Dave beamed. "I expect it will be easier to fix than I thought."

"Great!" said Mom. "I'd like to buy it when it's all fixed up."

Snuffy was so overjoyed that Mom could hardly wheel him from the store.

Soon Dave called to say Vroom-Vroom was ready. The whole family went to get him—even Snuffy.

After that, Snuffy never forgot to be open-hearted and kind. He had learned to love and care for all his friends and family. He even had gratitude in his heart for dirt, crumbs, and dust bunnies… and especially the button that had brought his brother and him back together again.

He was happy.

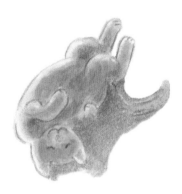

THE END